MAXIMUS
Rides Again

MAXIMUS
Rides Again

Brian Ogden

Illustrated by Elke Counsell

Scripture Union

By the same author
Maximus Mouse
Maximus and The Great Expedition
Short Tails and Tall Stories

Maximus colour books
Maximus and the lettuce thieves
Maximus and the television
Maximus goes on holiday
Maximus has a bad day

© Brian Ogden
First published 1993
Reprinted 1995, 1996

Scripture Union, 207–209 Queensway,
Bletchley, Milton Keynes, MK2 2EB, England.

ISBN 0 86201 834 X

British Library Cataloguing in Publication Data.
A catalogue record for this book is available from the
British Library.

Phototypeset by Apex Products, Singapore.
Printed and bound in Great Britain by Cox and Wyman Ltd,
Reading, Berkshire.

Contents

Maximus rides again

Since Maximus told me his first adventures we have had lots of letters from children and adults who seem to have enjoyed the first book of mousy happenings. Maximus is now older, but shows no signs of being any wiser, as you will find out. For those of you who have not met him before, I should explain that Maximus is a perfectly ordinary skateboarding mouse who lives in the vestry of St Michael's Church.

The first book – MAXIMUS MOUSE – has been used in school assemblies and has also been read to, or by, children at home. In the previous book Maximus took several nibbles at the Lord's Prayer. In this book he looks at some of the things that happen every day – like bullying or being ill or being jealous.

Maximus has several friends but the main one is Patrick, another mouse, who lives in the Sunday School cupboard. There are others including Barnabas, a very well-educated bat, and Sebastian Slow, a snail, who ends up as a football! Maximus isn't always a very nice mouse but then we are not always very nice people.

Both of us would like to thank all those who wrote to us and we do hope you will enjoy MAXIMUS RIDES AGAIN. We dedicate this book to Thomas and hope that he too will enjoy the stories when he is a little older.

Maximus Mouse and Brian Ogden

Maximus breaks the rules

'For goodness sake, Maximus, slow down,' shouted Patrick. 'You'll have a terrible accident any moment. STOP! MAXIMUS, STOP!'

The two mice, Maximus and his friend Patrick, were out in the graveyard of St Michael's Church. They had saved up to buy a skateboard. It was ten centimetres long and they had painted it luminous green. They had found an old piece of wood fallen from the fence, and leant it against a gravestone to make a ramp. Maximus climbed the ramp, jumped onto the skateboard and, with a shout of 'Geronimouse!', came hurtling down the ramp and landed on his nose in the soft grass.

'Ouch! In fact, double ouch!' cried Maximus, rubbing his nose with his front paws. 'That hurts. But did you see me go? Must have been faster than Tom chasing Jerry.'

'I do think we should read the booklet,' suggested Patrick. 'It said on the box, "Read Rules Before Starting". Here we are, now what do they say?'

7

And this is what Patrick read.

1. Never skateboard without a hard hat.
2. Always wear pads on your knees and elbows.
3. Make sure you know where you will land if you jump.
4. Do not skateboard where there are other animals.

'You're a spoil-sport,' said Maximus. 'We're only trying it out. Hey, are you going to have your go?'

'Not until we've got the right gear,' said Patrick. 'Let's go and sort out what we need now.'

'Oh, OK then. Bet I can go even faster next time.'

The two friends carried the board between them back into the church. They put it down in the vestry, which is where Maximus lives, and started to make knee pads from a piece of grubby paper handkerchief which the organist had dropped.

'What are we going to do about helmets?' asked Maximus.

'Well, I've had an idea about that. Do you remember those walnuts we had the other day? I reckon the shells would make perfect crash hats!'

'Brilliant,' replied Maximus. 'Can't wait to try one on. Come on, let's go and get them.'

The two mice scampered out of the vestry and ran round to the dustbin. They scrambled up the side and started to search for the walnut shells. After looking through some very smelly flowers, some very soggy tea bags and some service sheets they found what they were looking for − two shells. They scooped out the middle bits and then tried them on.

'Great! Couldn't be better,' said Patrick. 'Quick! Let's get out! I can hear the dustmen coming.' Just in time the two mice jumped to the ground clutching their shells and ran back to the church. 'Well,' said Patrick, 'I must go and have supper with Paula and the children. See you in the morning.'

Maximus went back to the vestry and saw the gleaming skateboard. He walked all the way round it, admiring the bright paint, the shining silver-coloured wheels, the names they had painted on the side — Speedie Max and Pushing Pat. 'Pity not to try it again,' he said out loud. 'Be safe enough in the church.' He put all four paws firmly on the ground and pushed as hard as he could with his shoulder. The little skateboard moved slowly out of the vestry and into the church.

Maximus looked round for a slope. There were two steps down into the nave of the church. Maximus grabbed some hymn books and made a slope on the steps. He stepped onto the skateboard and began to push hard with one paw. The board moved slowly forward, and then faster and then faster still. Maximus was just managing to keep his balance, when the board dropped over the step onto the hymn books and then down again onto the nave floor. By this time the skateboard was going so fast that it was all that Maximus could do to hang on with all four paws.

In the distance he could see the font right at the end of the aisle. It got bigger and bigger as Maximus got nearer and nearer. By this time he was yelling at the top of his voice, 'Help! Help! Please somemouse help me!'

At the moment that Maximus crashed into the stone base of the font, Patrick came running out of the Sunday School cupboard.

'What are you doing? Have you hurt yourself? What's more, have you hurt my skateboard?'

Maximus just lay at the foot of the font, moaning loudly and holding his head with his paws. Patrick went over to him. Maximus opened one eye and looked up.

'I've broken my head,' he said. 'I'm sure I've split it in two . . . oh, oh, oh.'

'Where, may I ask, is your crash nut?' demanded Patrick. 'You deserve a broken head for not wearing it. Mice who break rules get into trouble.' But he helped Maximus back to the vestry and put him to bed.

The next morning Maximus woke up with a terrible headache. He felt bruised all over and had a really black eye. When Patrick came in to see him, Maximus was a very quiet and sorry-for-himself mouse.

'I'm really sorry,' said Maximus. 'I promise you I will always keep the rules in future — wear my crash nut and the protectors.'

Patrick forgave him and repainted the skateboard where Maximus had scratched it. They had lots of fun but always kept to the rules and never got hurt again.

Heavenly Father,
You have given us rules to live by which are meant to protect us. Help us to keep them. Most of all, may we love you and love our friends. Amen.

Race against time

Maximus was sulking. He had gone off by himself down into the cellar where the heating boiler was kept. It was very hot and there was a roaring noise from the boiler — neither of which made him feel any better! The trouble was he was jealous of Patrick.

'He can skateboard better than me. He can run faster than me. He's always right! He always knows what's best. Why can't I be best sometimes?'

This super sulk had come about over a skateboard challenge. Maximus had challenged Patrick to a skateboard race. St Michael's Church was on an island surrounded completely by roads. It was quite a long way round the whole church and churchyard, and Maximus had suggested that they race around the island. Because they only had one skateboard it had to be a race against the clock.

Maximus was quite sure that he would win. He dressed up in the knee and elbow pads, put the crash nut on his head and waited for the church clock to strike. The moment the first boom rang out he set off pushing hard on the road with his front paws, first the left and then the right. Away from the churchyard gate, bouncing over a drain cover, just missing a Coke can lying in the gutter, he sped round the churchyard wall. He took no notice of the road junction and just hoped there were no human cars coming. He turned the corner and there in front of him was a hole. Workmen had been digging up the road and left a barrier round it at human waist height – not much good for stopping skateboarding mice. In he tumbled, his paws came off the board and he nose-dived into the soft mud. For a moment or two he wasn't sure where he was, then he grabbed the board and staggered up out of the hole, shaking off the mud and small stones. He thought of giving up but decided against it. He jumped back on the board and raced on down the road.

By the back entrance to the churchyard he saw a small dog out of the corner of his eye. The animal thought this was great fun and started to bark and run by the side of the speeding mouse. An old lady going to the church couldn't believe her eyes – a black and white terrier trotting alongside a skateboarding mouse! What was the world coming to?

Maximus was getting out of breath. He had gone most of the way around the churchyard and could see Patrick standing by the main entrance – the finishing line – looking up at the clock. As he got nearer he could hear Patrick saying, 'Eleven minutes, eleven and a half minutes, twelve . . .'

'NOW,' yelled Maximus, panting hard as he crossed the gateway. He fell off the board and lay for a long time on the grass before he could speak. 'Bet you can't beat that!' he boasted to Patrick. But Patrick, who knew about the hole in the road, got round the course in ten and a half minutes.

The result of the race had been the final straw. Maximus just managed a bad tempered 'You won –

but it wasn't fair, you knew about the hole.' Then he stamped off down to the cellar muttering to himself.

'He does everything better than me. I never win anything. I wish I was good at something. It's not fair. I'm just a useless mouse who can't ever get anything right.'

After an hour or so, while Maximus got hotter and hotter and dustier and dustier, he heard paw steps coming down the stairs to the cellar. 'Nobody ever leaves me in peace,' muttered Maximus in a squeak loud enough to be heard.

'Er, Maximus?' asked Patrick.

'Course it is. Who else did you think it was — Father Chrismouse?' replied Maximus rudely.

'Maximus,' said Patrick again. 'Please come out of here. Paula and I want you to come to tea.'

'I'm not hungry,' said Maximus, telling a lie. He was very hungry after the race, and very thirsty having been in the hot cellar.

'Please come,' begged Patrick. 'The children want to see you.'

'All right then,' said Maximus. 'If the children want to see me, I'll come. But I must have a shower first. Be round in about half an hour.' Both mice climbed up out of the cellar and Maximus went to the vestry where he washed and changed.

It was quite quiet and dark as Maximus crawled through the hole into the Sunday School cupboard. Suddenly he heard a voice saying 'NOW!' At that moment the light went on and a hundred voices started to sing 'For he's a jolly good Maximus'.

Paula had cooked a lovely meal — grilled organ music with candle wax sauce and for pudding, banana skin with ice cream. Just before they started to eat, Patrick stood up.

'You may not remember, Maximus, but today is a very special day for all of us. It was one year ago today that

you were very kind to a poor hungry mouse who came through a hole into your vestry. That mouse was me and you invited me to bring Paula and the family into the church. We have been so happy here and it's all due to you. You are the kindest mouse I know. I wish I was as kind and generous as you.'

Maximus couldn't believe his furry ears. Here was Patrick wishing he was actually like Maximus! Perhaps after all he was good at something — being kind to other mice. They had a wonderful party and Maximus played games with the children until well past their bedtime. Their favourite was Postmouse's Knock and all the children gave Maximus a big kiss.

Heavenly Father,
It is so easy to be jealous of other people — for what they have or for what they can do. Thank you for making us as we are. Help us to make the best of ourselves. Amen.

Maximus and Uncle Clarence

'They're not very nice when they get old, you know,' said Maximus to Patrick. 'They shout and can't hear. They moan all the time about how good it used to be and how dreadful it is now – how the cost of cheese has gone up and how young mice behave today.'

The two mice were having a chat about some of the old mice they knew. Maximus had an uncle who lived in a special home for elderly rodents. Maximus had not seen the old mouse for a long time and Patrick had suggested that he ought to visit his uncle again.

'Yes, I know all that. My grandfather was just the same,' replied Patrick. 'He used to fall asleep whilst I was talking to him. But I do think you should go and see Uncle Clarence. Why not go tomorrow? Don't forget to take him a little present.'

Maximus did not want to spend a whole day visiting his old uncle but he got up early, left St Michael's Church and caught the bus to the town where his uncle lived. He stopped off at the newsagent to buy a book about the President of the United States, called The White Mouse, which he thought that his uncle might enjoy reading. As he got closer to the home, which was called The Mouse Keeper, he began to think about his uncle. It couldn't be much fun being very old. You couldn't scamper about any more, or play games. You would need other mice to help you get dressed and perhaps even to help you to eat and wash.

Maximus walked slowly up the drive and could see a number of elderly mice sitting in their wheelchairs in the warm sun. There were some pretty lady mice in white uniforms pushing the chairs around the beautiful garden. Maximus thought he recognised his uncle in a wheelchair and went over to see. Sure enough, it was Uncle Clarence.

'Hullo there, young Maximus,' said Clarence. 'It's good to see you. This young lady', and he turned round to look at the nurse mouse pushing his chair, 'is Maxine. This is my nephew Maximus.'

'It's very good to see you, Maximus,' said Maxine. 'I have often heard your uncle talk about you.'

Maximus was beginning to feel dreadful. His uncle had talked about him to this pretty nurse but it had taken him ages to come and visit the old mouse. He really should have paid a visit before now.

'Er, by the way, Uncle, I've brought you this book to read,' said Maximus. 'I do hope you like it.' Maximus put the book on the wheelchair. Just at that moment a loud bell rang.

'You've arranged that well,' said Clarence. 'It's time for lunch – are you going to join us for a nibble? The cheese is very good here – well matured.'

Maximus pushed Clarence into the house and ate a very good lunch. His uncle had been right – the cheese was really fantastic and cooked just the way Maximus liked it. The two chatted away over lunch and then went to Clarence's room.

18

'You know, Maximus, you really do look very much like your grandfather, Arthur,' suggested Clarence. The old mouse pointed to a dusty portrait hanging on the wall above his bed. The mouse was dressed in what seemed to Maximus to be very old-fashioned clothes. He had whiskers which stuck straight out sideways and was wearing a bowler hat. Maximus could not see why his uncle thought he looked like his grandfather.

'Uncle, please tell me more about him,' asked Maximus. 'My father always said that Arthur was somemouse very special.'

'Well, it's all a long time ago now but I do remember that Arthur, who was my father as well as your father's father, did have a very exciting life. He loved to play jokes on people. There was the time when he was living in the Theatre Royal. It was just after Christmas and the pantomime was Cinderella. The good fairy was waving her wand and saying, "Cinderella, you shall go to the Ball". Arthur took the place of the toy rat who was changed into a pony to pull the carriage for Cinderella. Cinderella saw Arthur waggle his whiskers at her and did she yell! Both Cinderella and the good fairy ran screaming off the stage. I'm afraid Arthur was told to move out of the theatre after that!'

'What a wonderful story! I bet he was really popular,' said Maximus. 'I'm sure my dad told me how Grandfather Arthur scared the cat in *Puss in Boots*. I think he was living in another theatre then?'

'Quite right, my boy,' replied his uncle. 'The family have always liked the theatre. I think you mean the time when Arthur and your grandmother Sally rented a mouse hole in the Royal Box at the Palladium. It was a performance of *Dick Whittington*, the boy who came to London with his cat and later became Lord Mayor. Arthur and Sally had gone down from the Royal Box to the edge of the stage to get a better look at the cat. It seems strange to us but humans like dressing up and a very small female human plays the part of the cat in the pantomime.'

'Those are the ones who don't like us, aren't they, uncle?' asked Maximus.

'Well,' said Clarence, 'they do tend to jump about and scream when they see us. That was the problem in *Dick Whittington*. Dick and the cat were in the middle of the pantomime – just when it was quiet, when the cat saw Arthur and Sally. She leapt in the air and fell off the stage into the orchestra pit, landing on the big drum. Once again Arthur and Sally had to leave the theatre rather quickly!'

'I think that your uncle has had enough excitement for one day,' said Maxine. 'Why don't you come back again next week and have another chat?'

'That's a really good idea,' said Maximus. 'I would love to know more about my family. Goodbye, Uncle Clarence.' But his uncle had already fallen asleep. Maximus tip-pawed out and caught the bus home.

'Well, how was it?' asked Patrick. 'Were you bored stiff?'

'No, I have to be honest,' said Maximus. 'I really enjoyed seeing Uncle Clarence. He's got some wonderful stories about the family. I might write a book of them. We could call it *Mouse Tales*.'

'That's dreadful,' said Patrick. 'Now go to bed.'

Heavenly Father,
Thank you for our families. Thank you for their love and for what we can learn from them. Help us to care about old people, especially those who are lonely or ill, and to do what we can to help them. Amen.

Maximus is lonely

Maximus was wandering about the church feeling sorry for himself. Patrick, together with Paula and the children, had gone off on holiday leaving Maximus on his own. They had begged him to come with them. 'You know how the children love playing games with you,' they said. 'There's lots of room in the holiday camp — you'd love Mutlins.' But Maximus didn't really like the sea. It frightened him. All that water everywhere, sand in everything, and crowds of mice all fighting for a place by the pool, putting towels out early to reserve a sun bed. He had decided to stay at home by himself and now he wished he hadn't.

'There's nobody about. Even old Barnabas the bat has flown off to the Isle of Batman. I'm fed up,' muttered Maximus as he kicked at the hassocks, the large kneelers that some humans use when they say their prayers. He didn't even notice when some delicious-looking stuffing came out of one.

'I shall go bananas if I don't find somemouse to squeak to soon.' Then he had an idea. Why not go and see Uncle

Clarence again? At least he would be somemouse to talk to, and he had enjoyed the last visit.

After the bus journey he walked up the path into the home for elderly rodents and wondered if he would see that nice nurse Maxine again. There was nobody about in the garden, so he went straight to Uncle Clarence's room. Just as he was about to knock on the door he heard a squeak — it was Maxine.

'Hullo,' she said, 'it's Maximus, isn't it? I'm afraid that your uncle is having a sleep at the moment. He hasn't been too well. Oh dear, I expect you've come rather a long way to visit him?'

'Well,' answered Maximus, 'yes, I have. Perhaps I can wait and see him later?'

'Why not come and have some Maxwell Mouse coffee with me? I'm due for a break.'

So off went Maximus and Maxine to the staff lounge. Maximus soon realised that Maxine was a long way from home. She had come down from the north to find work and didn't really know anyone in the area. She was as lonely as he was. They had a long chat. Maximus told her all about his work at St Michael's Church and Maxine told him how she looked after the old rodents in the home. Before he went to see his uncle, Maximus invited the mouse nurse to come over to St Michael's Church on her day off.

'Sorry I was asleep when you came,' said Uncle Clarence who was very pleased to see his nephew again. 'I haven't felt too fit since you came last time. I've had to stay in bed and it has given me a lot of time to think. You asked me lots of questions before about the family. Families are very important, you know, Maximus. Your grandfather Arthur used to quote an old rhyme. It went like this, "Mice who are best together, are those who nest together." You're never lonely with a family near you.'

'I shall come and see you again soon, Uncle,' said Maximus. 'I must scamper off now or I shall miss the bus.' He had enjoyed his visit to Uncle Clarence and went home feeling much better. He didn't feel lonely any more but was excited because he had Maxine's visit to look forward to on the following Saturday.

Maximus spent all Saturday morning dusting, polishing, sweeping and tidying his space in the vestry. He kept running out of the church to look at the church clock. He couldn't wait to see Maxine again and show her round St Michael's. Just as he began to think she wasn't coming, he heard a noise at the back of the church, and there she was. Maximus proudly showed her the font where he had nearly drowned, the organ which he had put out of tune, and finally the vestry where he lived. Maxine seemed very interested and the two mice didn't stop talking all day.

'It's funny but now I have met you I don't feel lonely any more,' said Maxine shyly, 'I've really enjoyed today.'

'It's been great,' said Maximus. 'I know I'm lucky I've got Patrick as a friend, but he does have Paula and all their children. I know how you feel about loneliness. Everyone needs somemouse special. But you do have to make an effort — you can be lonely forever if you don't do something about it. You have to do it — you can't leave it to others. Perhaps we can meet again?'

'Oh, I do hope so,' said Maxine. 'Will you be over again to see your uncle?'

'I certainly will,' said Maximus. 'Would next Thursday be a good day?'

Heavenly Father,
When we are lonely help us to talk to you, just as Jesus did when he felt alone. When we see others who are lonely help us to be friends with them. Amen.

Maximus goes to hospital

'Oh, ow, oh, ow,' groaned Maximus as he tossed and turned in his bed. 'Oh my poor tummy! Oh my poor head! Oh poor me!'

Maximus had not had a good night. He had been awake most of the time and had heard every hour strike on the church clock. His tummy ache had started just after the clock struck two and wasn't any better when it struck three, four, five or six. At seven o'clock he lay there hoping that Patrick or Paula or one of their children would come into the vestry.

The minutes ticked by and Maximus was feeling worse. His head felt hot, his tummy seemed to have at least two teams playing football inside it and, when he tried to stand up, his legs wouldn't do what they were told. At last he heard the sound of paws outside the vestry door.

'Can I come in?' asked Paula. 'Oh dear, whatever's the matter, Maximus? You look dreadful.'

'I feel dreadful. There isn't one bit of me that feels right. It all aches. I think I need a doctor.'

'Yes, I can see that,' said Paula. 'I'll ask Patrick to get him at once.' She went quickly out of the vestry leaving Maximus groaning in his paper hanky duvet.

After what seemed ages to Maximus, the door opened again and in came Paula with the doctor. 'I'm Doctor What. I'm afraid that Doctor Who couldn't come today. What seems to be the matter, Mr Maximus?'

'I've got terrible pains, doctor,' moaned Maximus. 'My tummy has been fighting itself all night, my head feels like the football in a cup final and I've got aches where I didn't think things could ache. Er . . . I'm not well, doctor.'

The doctor tried not to laugh at what Maximus had said. He rolled up Maximus' nightshirt and put his paws on Maximus' tummy.

'Oh,' groaned Maximus, 'ever so oh!'

'What's the matter?' asked the doctor. 'Did that hurt?'

'No,' said Maximus. 'It's just that your paws are cold!'

'Sorry about that, but you must tell me where the pain is. Does that hurt?'

'Yes, yes, yes!' shouted Maximus.

The doctor listened to Maximus' breathing through his stethoscope, which is the long tube doctors put in their ears and on someone's back and tummy to hear what is going on inside. He asked Maximus to say 'Ah' and looked into his eyes.

'I'm sorry to say but you have got food poisoning. You must have eaten something bad. I'm going to have to send you to hospital for a few days until you're better.'

The doctor went off to telephone the ambulance and arrange for a bed in the hospital. Paula, looking quite worried, stayed with Maximus.

'I don't want to go to hospital,' whispered Maximus. 'Paula, I'm frightened of hospitals. I might never come home again. I don't want to go. Please don't let them take me.'

27

'What ever happened to that brave mouse I used to know?' asked Paula, trying to be cheerful. 'Maximus, old friend, you're going to be all right. If the doctor says "hospital", then you must go. Patrick and the children and me too, all want you better. I promise we will come and visit you. Now let's get you ready to go.' And Paula packed a little case for Maximus with his toothbrush, toothpaste, clean underclothes and a new nightshirt.

The ambulance mice were very kind to Maximus. They put him gently on a stretcher, covered him with a tissue and carried him out to the ambulance. Very soon they were at the hospital where Maximus was wheeled into a ward with lots of beds. He was lifted onto one of the empty beds and a young nurse mouse, looking very smart in her blue uniform, came over to talk to him.

'Hullo. It's Mr Maximus, isn't it?' she asked in a friendly voice. 'I'm going to put all your things away in this cupboard and in a few minutes a doctor will come and have a good look at you. There's really nothing to worry about — she's a very good doctor.'

Almost before his clean underwear was in the drawer the lady doctor came to see Maximus. She was dressed in a white coat and had a stethoscope hanging out of one pocket. She gently pulled up Maximus' pyjama top and began to examine his tummy. 'Tell me where it hurts, please, Mr Maximus,' she said. 'I hear from your doctor that he thinks you have food poisoning — we'll soon get that cleared up and get you home again.'

Maximus was already beginning to feel a little happier. Everyone had been so kind to him and he wasn't feeling nearly so frightened. Before the doctor went away she told him that he would have to take some rather nasty tasting medicine. Very soon the nurse came back with a huge bottle. On the side were the letters M.T.C.

'Excuse me, nurse, but what does M.T.C. stand for?' asked Maximus.

The nurse laughed and said, 'IT stands for "Mouse Tummy Cure". It's the best medicine for mice with poorly tummies. Now open wide.'

The moment Maximus began to open his mouth the nurse filled it with a large spoonful of M.T.C. Poor Maximus thought that he had never tasted anything so dreadful in his life. First it seemed to burn the roof of his mouth, then it set fire to his throat and then it felt as if his tongue was wearing gloves. It was thick and yellow, and stuck in his teeth and on his whiskers. It tasted like muddy water with rotting leaves, or was it very old cheese with blue mould? Maximus couldn't make up his mind.

Slowly he began to close his eyes and relax in the bed. Before much longer he was fast asleep and the M.T.C. began to do its work. When he woke up several hours later he heard voices that he knew.

'There you are, Maximus. I promised we'd come and see you,' said Paula. 'They would only let Patrick and me come in — we've left the children outside. How are you feeling now?'

'Well, I think I'm feeling a bit better,' said Maximus. 'They have been so kind in here — and Paula, I'm not frightened of hospitals any more. I am looking forward to coming home but I shall never be afraid of doctors or nurses again.'

Just at that moment the nurse came to take Maximus' temperature and Patrick and Paula went home. Maximus had a good night's sleep and after only another two days was allowed home. When he walked into the vestry he had such a surprise. Stretched over the mouse hole was a banner which read 'Welcome Home Maximus'. After that he was much more careful what he ate — he didn't want any more M.T.C. ever again!

Heavenly Father,
It can be frightening when we are ill. We ask you to be close to all those people who are unwell. We pray that you will help all those who work to make others well. Amen.

Weight on his mind

It was the sort of day that seemed good from the moment that Maximus woke up. He stretched each leg and each paw slowly one by one. He yawned, rubbed his eyes, twirled his whiskers and looked round the vestry. The sun, which had been awake long before Maximus, was shining brightly through the high stained-glass windows, making coloured patterns on the wall. It was a good day to be alive. A day to do exciting things. A day to remember.

At last Maximus rolled out of his handkerchief duvet and folded it neatly before putting it away in his cupboard. He took two pieces of special candle from his cupboard and wandered happily about the church nibbling at these. They had been made from less fattening wax and written on each were the words, 'Can help slimming only as part of a calorie controlled diet'.

'This is the day,' said Maximus to an empty church. 'This is the tomorrow I talked about yesterday. I am starting today. I am going to count every calorie – no more fattening hymnburgers, no more biscuit crumbs, no more crisps, no more chocolate. There is going to be less of me from now on. I almost got stuck in that old mouse hole. All my clothes have shrunk. I will only eat the right food from now on.'

Maximus had been putting on too much weight. He got out of breath running up the aisle of the church. Worst of all, other mice were saying rude things about him. Patrick had talked about large mouse shadows on the wall. Paula had said to her children before one meal, 'Now, children, don't eat too much or you will get like your Uncle Maximus.'

'Right,' said Maximus. 'After breakfast I'm going jogging.' He went back to the vestry and put on his track suit and a pair of very expensive trainers. 'Now I must remember to warm up first,' he said. Very gently he lifted his two front paws above his head and started to jog on the spot. Then he stood with his hind paws apart and swung his front paws by his side. 'Fine,' he panted, 'no trouble at all. Soon be really fit . . . er, perhaps I ought to sit down for a moment before beginning the jog.' And he sat down on his duvet, sweat pouring down his whiskers, with his head in his paws. 'I think I was meant to be a well built mouse – not one of those anoratic ones you can't see sideways!'

In a few minutes Maximus was feeling better and, after a reviving drink, he crept out of the vestry and looked carefully around the church. 'Good,' he said, 'no one there. Perhaps I could jog to the font and back?' He jumped down the steps into the nave of the church and, with his head held high, jogged steadily down the aisle towards the font. Although he was out of breath by the time he reached it, he didn't stop and turned straight round for the return journey. He passed pew after pew – the bench-like seats that humans sit on – going slower and slower. By the time he reached the front row his heart was racing and he was gasping for breath.

'Oh dear, oh dear,' he panted, as he lay on the floor. 'It's worse than I thought. It's no good. I shall have to join Weight Watchers Anonymouse. Paula was right.'

That very evening Maximus left the church and scampered off down the road to the Weight Watchers meeting. He rather shyly peeped round the door and looked in to see who else was there. There were a couple of overweight hedgehogs who complained that their prickles felt tight. In one corner were three frogs who croaked, 'We've lost our hop! We can't take off and our friends say that it's because we are too heavy.'

In another corner was a lonely hamster. Maximus decided to go and talk to her. 'I've never been the same since having the twins,' said Hilda Hamster. 'I put on so much weight then that I keep getting stuck in things. It's so embarrassing. I was crawling in the kitchen yesterday and got wedged into a coffee mug on its side. I went in to lick the sugar off the bottom and couldn't turn round. I had to roll the mug off the table and creep away when it smashed on the floor.'

'A very nasty experience for you,' sympathised Maximus. 'I know how you feel — I had to get my best friend to pull me out of a jar when I got strawberry-jammed the other day.'

At that moment a very slim and healthy looking rabbit spoke loudly. 'My name', she said, 'is Hortense. I am your leader. Fellow sufferers,' she continued, 'gather round now and pay attention. Welcome to this meeting of Weight Watchers. It is a great pleasure to welcome some new members who have been living off the fat of the land. You have already done the hardest part of losing weight — you have been brave enough to come here tonight. This evening I shall tell you about the Weight Watchers PLAN. But firstly we need to weigh everyone and then tell you your ideal weight.'

By the time that they had all been weighed and told how much they should really be, Maximus was getting tired – and hungry. He said goodbye to Hilda and promised he would see her next week and went off home. The church was in darkness by the time he got there, so he struggled through the hole into the vestry unable to see anything. He stopped by the wall and sniffed. There was a certain something in the vestry which had definitely not been there when he left. He raised his nose in the air and sniffed again. Not only was there something new but something that smelled delicious. It was sort of sweet and chewy and nutty and chocolate and, and . . . he had to have some. He moved slowly in the blackness of the vestry towards the most beautiful smell he had ever sniffed. Whatever it was, was wrapped in paper. He tore at the paper with all four paws, rolling around on the floor, fighting the wrapping which was keeping him away from the smell. At last the wrapping fell away and Maximus sank his front teeth into a piece of chocolate nut fudge. Bliss – perfect bliss.

As the last morsel disappeared Maximus had a thought. *As members of Weight Watchers you will not eat any biscuits or cake or, most of all, any sweets.* The words of Hortense came back to him. Already he was a failure. How could he face the other Weight Watchers next week at the weigh-in? He would be the only one who had failed. The only one who had put on more weight. The only one who had given in to temptation. What a miserable mouse he was!

The next morning Patrick came into the vestry and Maximus confessed what had happened. 'We love you as you are,' said Patrick, 'but we know you need to lose some weight. I'll jog with you and help keep you away from sweets. Soon you'll be a star member of Weight Watchers and show up all the others.'

Heavenly Father,
We often do what we shouldn't do and fail to do what
we should. Help us to know what is right and give us the
strength to do it. Amen.

A game of footsnail

'Stop it, please stop it,' begged the snail. 'I'm getting dizzy. You're hurting me. Please stop.'

But Maximus and Patrick took no notice of the little creature and continued to kick it.

'It's my turn in goal,' said Maximus. 'You've been in for ages.' The two mice swopped over. The goal posts were two hymn books standing on the church floor. Maximus was wearing his Mousehampton United shirt and his best trainers. Patrick dribbled the snail shell round a flower stand and took a mighty kick. The poor snail shot over Maximus' head and landed with a crash against a hassock.

'That's your worst shot yet,' laughed Maximus. 'Thought we were playing football, not basket ball!'

The snail, whose name was Sebastian (named after the famous athlete snail – Sebastian Slow), pushed his head out of his shell. He shook it from side to side to make sure his neck was still working and then began to slide away as quietly and quickly as possible.

'I don't think our creepy friend wants to play any more,' said Patrick. 'I don't think he likes football.'

'Oh, let him go,' said Maximus. 'Some creatures are just not born to be great footballers like me. It's time we had a rest. Come on, let's see what we can find to eat.'

The two mice had been playing football in the church, using Sebastian as the football, even though he had begged them not to do it. They walked out of the church into the bright sunshine, chatting about the game.

'Great shot that last one of yours,' said Maximus. 'It went so high I bet Sebastian wished he'd had a parachute!'

'You're not much better,' replied his friend. 'You kicked him into the flower vase and nearly drowned him!'

The mice wandered around between the gravestones, kicking pebbles to each other and boasting about their football skills. They did not notice the large white eyes looking down from the church tower, nor see the sharp claws, nor the grey black feathers ruffling in the breeze. With barely a sound, John and Doris, the two jackdaws who nested in the tower, swooped down and snatched the mice in their feet.

Before either Maximus or Patrick could say 'Cheddar cheese' they were off the ground hanging beneath the two birds. The mice were terrified – one minute happily kicking about in the churchyard and the next flying above the church, held far too tightly for comfort by the sharp claws of the jackdaws. For what seemed ages the mice were speechless. There was nothing they could do. The claws were holding them very firmly and even if they wriggled clear they would fall to the ground.

At last Maximus got his voice back. 'Help! Help!' he squeaked. 'You're hurting me. Please stop. Please put us down.'

'Now where have I heard that before?' asked John as he continued to fly round the churchyard in a large circle.

'Well, dear,' replied his wife, only a wing tip away. 'I seem to remember hearing it inside the church not very long ago. I think it was a poor frightened snail who was talking.'

'And I remember seeing two macho mice bravely kicking a snail about.'

'I think we'd better land and talk about this,' suggested Doris.

The two birds, with their cargoes of scared mice, landed on a ledge on the church tower. They put the mice down unhurt on the ledge. Maximus immediately put his paws to his eyes.

'I'm going to be sick,' he said. 'I can't stand heights. I get frightened on a thick carpet.'

It was Patrick who came to his senses, even though he was shaking with fear.

'Please, sir,' he said, looking at John Jackdaw and trying not to look down at the ground far below. 'Please, sir, what are you going to do with us?'

'We haven't quite decided yet,' said the jackdaw, fluttering his wings to stay on the draughty ledge. 'You do understand that we jackdaws rather fancy a meal of mice. My wife has lots of mice recipes.'

'Yes,' said Doris Jackdaw, 'John likes fried mice and I'm very fond of mice pudding!'

'But . . . but . . . but we're church mice; we never do anybody any harm.'

'That's not what we saw and heard,' said Doris. 'You were being very cruel to Sebastian, kicking him about the church and laughing when he asked you to stop.'

'We're really sorry,' said Patrick.

'We'll never do it again, I promise,' said Maximus.

'We didn't mean to hurt him,' added Patrick. 'I hope he's all right.'

'Well, on this occasion we might just let you go,' said John. 'But let this be a warning to you. Never bully smaller creatures than yourselves. You don't like being frightened and neither do they.'

Once more the two mice were fastened tight by the claws of the jackdaws. The birds took off from the tower ledge and landed gracefully back in the churchyard. The mice shook themselves, glad to be free, and scampered into the church, having learnt a lesson.

Heavenly Father,
We pray for all those children and adults in the world who are bullied by others. Help us to support them by our friendship and give us the courage to challenge those who are bullies. Amen.

Barnabas to the rescue

'I won't let them do it,' shouted Maximus. 'They have no right to do it. It's *my* vestry. I live here, not them.'

'Calm down, Maximus, before you blow your whiskers off,' said Patrick. 'It isn't your vestry, it belongs to the church.'

The problem had started when Maximus picked up a copy of the church magazine. He was hoping to have a couple of pages for breakfast — he found the vicar's letter was always quite tasty — when he saw a headline which read 'New Vestry To Be Built'. Having difficulty with some of the longer words, he asked Patrick, who had paid much more attention at mouse school, to help him read it.

Patrick read, 'The church council has decided to pull down the old vestry and build a hall by the side of the church in its place. This will make room for our Sunday School and other meetings.' It was this news which had made Maximus so angry.

'It may belong to the church, but I have lived here for years and years. They haven't asked me what I think about it. Why do they need to start changing everything?

Whatever is wrong with it as it is? That's it, they don't want me any more. Fine lot they are!'

'Maximus, that isn't right. Of course they want you but the church needs a larger hall. They have to knock down the old vestry to make room for the new building.'

'Well, I shall leave and let them look after the church without me. Then they'll find out what it's like without a guard mouse. Then they'll be sorry.' And Maximus stormed off, kicking his paws against anything he could find. He turned round and shouted to Patrick, 'I'm going to pack.'

As Maximus disappeared into the vestry Patrick scampered off to the west end of the church and started to climb the steps up into the tower. About halfway up is the belfry where the church bells hang. There is also something, or rather someone else, who hangs in the belfry. That someone is Barnabas, the church bat. Barnabas sleeps most of the day in the belfry and wakes up at night when he flies around keeping an eye on the whole place. Barnabas is clever. He has been to the B.U. (Bat University) and knows lots about belfries and batteries, which is where bats live. The mice always ask Barnabas' advice when they have a problem.

Patrick climbed into the belfry and looked around for Barnabas. It was usually quite difficult to find the little bat but Patrick soon saw him hanging upside down near the window.

'Well, what do you want now?' asked Barnabas, sounding rather bat tempered. 'I suppose it's some little thing that you mice can't sort out for yourselves. Where's that friend of yours, Minibus, or whatever his name is?'

'Please, Mr Barnabas,' said Patrick, 'it's Maximus that's the problem. You see, the church people are going to knock down the vestry and Maximus thinks he won't have anywhere to live and that they don't want him any more and he is packing up to leave and I don't want him to leave and please, Mr Barnabas, you must do something.'

45

'Calm down, Pea Stick, or whatever your name is,' ordered Barnabas. 'You say the church people are going to change the vestry into a big hall. I expect you two mice are getting your whiskers in a twist over nothing as usual. I suppose I shall have to sort it all out for you or I shan't get any peace. Leave it to me.'

'Oh, thank you,' said Patrick gratefully. 'I can stop Maximus and tell him it's all right then?'

'Yes, off you go and let me work out what to do. Don't fall down the stairs.' And the bat flew up to a bell rope and hung silently upside down to think.

Patrick tumbled down the steps of the tower, picked himself up at the bottom and scampered off through the church towards the vestry. Just as he reached the door he ran straight into Maximus who was carrying a large paper bag over one shoulder. The two mice collided and Maximus dropped the bag. It burst open and out fell all Maximus' clothes, his designer jeans, his trainers, his duvet, his Mouse Maintenance book and some rather unhappy looking hymnburgers.

'You can't go,' panted Patrick. 'I won't let you go. I've seen Barnabas — he says he will sort it out.'

'Barnabas! What can he do?' asked Maximus. 'He's only a silly bat. He can't stop the humans from knocking down my home, can he?'

'Just give him a chance. Please, Maximus,' begged Patrick. 'Just see if there is anything he can do. If you rush off now we may never see you again.'

At that moment, with the pile of his belongings in his paws, Maximus's nose started to twitch. His whiskers wobbled and his mouth fell open. 'Is that smell what I think it is?' he asked. 'Is it really baked sermon notes?'

'Yes, you're right,' said Patrick thankfully. 'Paula said she was going to have a special lunch today as it's the twins' birthday.'

46

'But you've got eleven sets of twins,' said Maximus.

'That's why it's a special lunch, Maximus,' replied his friend, 'and you are invited.'

'Well . . . I suppose I could postpone leaving till after lunch. I always travel better on a full tummy.'

As the two mice got nearer to the Sunday School cupboard the delicious smell of baked sermon notes got stronger.

In the meantime Barnabas had come up with an idea. He flew out of the belfry window down towards the wooden hut where the workmen sat to have their tea and sandwiches, when they weren't digging the holes for the new hall. There were no humans about and he squeezed through the little window. There on a very rough table, with crumbs and spilt tea, was a copy of the plans for the new hall.

Barnabas, although a clever bat, wasn't too sure that he could get the plan right. He looked at it close to, and then flew above it, hovering like a helicopter. At last he had worked it out. The plan was fixed in his mind and he flew back to the church.

Meanwhile the mice were having a wonderful meal. Paula, who had trained as a mousekeeper, was a very good cook. The sermon notes had been baked to perfection and were served with some chopped hassock. Just as Maximus was thinking about having a third helping there was a banging at the window.

'It's Barnabas,' shouted all eleven pairs of twins together.

'Mr Barnabas to you,' said Paula. 'I wonder if he has any news? Come on, Patrick, open the window and let the poor bat in.'

Barnabas fluttered down to where the mice were eating. 'I have some interesting news for you all,' he said in a very important-sounding bat voice. 'I have been able to obtain the information that is required to deal with the matter of the ecclesiastical changing room known as the vestry.'

47

One of the twins whispered to Paula. 'What's he on about, Mum?'

'Shush, dear, listen to Mr Barnabas.'

The bat continued. 'As a result of my researches I can tell you quite bategorically that the humans intend building a new edifice juxtaposed to the ancient site of the current vestry. Included within this will be provision for all the functions previously exercised within the old vestry. Changes must come, for only with change can progress be maintained. We bats are far-sighted in matters of progress and adopt a more positive attitude than other less developed rodents.' With that he flew out of the window and back to the belfry.

'I didn't understand a word he said,' complained Maximus. 'What did he mean, Patrick?'

'I think what he meant, Maximus, was that when the humans build the new hall there is going to be a better vestry in it. There WILL be somewhere for you to live. It will be warmer and more comfortable. In fact, it is a change for the better and you should accept it and stay.'

'Well, perhaps I was a bit hasty,' said Maximus. 'I suppose it would be silly to go when I can have baked sermon notes here!'

Patrick and Paula and the eleven sets of twins all helped Maximus to collect his belongings together. He moved into the Sunday School cupboard with them until the new hall and vestry were finished.

Heavenly Father,
We like to keep things as they are — our friends, our school, our homes. Sometimes there have to be changes. Help us to learn from each change and to know that you never change. Amen.

Maximus says no

'I'm sure that Maximus will do it,' said Paula. 'He never minds looking after the children when we go out. Why don't you go and ask him?'

'Oh, all right,' replied her husband, Patrick. 'I'll see if he will. I'm really looking forward to the music − it's not often that Willy and the Whisker Bangers get to play gigs round here.' Patrick scampered off towards the vestry where Maximus was just struggling up out of his bed.

'Maximus, old friend, Paula and I wondered if you would do us a favour tonight?' asked Patrick. 'You see, we've got tickets for the Willy and the Whisker Bangers gig and we need a baby sitter. Any chance you can help?'

'Not tonight,' said Maximus, 'no, not tonight. You see it's my favourite telly tonight − it's *Coronation Mouseholes*. I never miss that. Sorry but you'll have to find someone else.'

Patrick went off feeling very disappointed, leaving Maximus to get washed and dressed.

A few moments later Maximus came out of the vestry and began to look around the church for some breakfast. It had been choir practice the night before and often a

page from an old hymnbook was left lying on the floor. Maximus loved a good hymn for his breakfast. Just as he had spotted a piece of paper lying under the organ stool he heard a strange sound. It felt like a draught, as though the window had suddenly opened on a windy day. He heard the flap of wings and, looking up, realised that it was Barnabas. Barnabas was the church bat who lived in the bell chamber.

'I say, you – er, Minibus, or whatever your name is,' said the bat, 'could you do me a favour? I've got a hospital appointment – got to have my batteries charged. I'm expecting a parcel in the post this afternoon. Would you mind taking it in for me?'

'No, not this afternoon,' said Maximus, 'no way, can't be done. I'm off skateboarding this afternoon. Got to get in practice for the return race with Patrick. You'll have to find someone else for your parcel.'

Barnabas flew off feeling very disappointed, leaving Maximus to dive under the organ stool for the hymn page. As it was a beautiful day Maximus went out into the church-yard whilst he chewed the hymn sheet. The sun was shining brightly, there wasn't a cloud in the sky, and Maximus sat down by a gravestone to finish off his breakfast.

Just as he reached the number at the bottom of the page there was a rustling sound and he saw the long grass sway-ing in front of him. After a moment a snout, followed by two eyes, followed by what looked like a large pin cushion, came out of the grass. It was Herbert the hedgehog.

'Ah, Maximus, just the mouse I was hoping to see,' said Herbert. 'You remember my daughter Henrietta, whom you saved from drowning in the pond? Well, she's just had a beautiful baby and she thought you would like to see her. The baby's name is Hyacinth Maximusa. We named her after you, because you saved Henrietta's life. Can you come and see her now before she goes home?'

'No, couldn't possibly,' said Maximus, 'the sun is just right for sunbathing on my favourite gravestone. I'm going to sunbathe on Dead Ernest right now.'

Herbert went off feeling very disappointed that Maximus didn't want to see his granddaughter and Maximus lay down in the hot sun and went to sleep.

Several hours later the sun hid behind the church tower and the gravestone was left in the shade. Maximus awoke with a shiver. He felt like the two taps in a wash basin — both hot and cold. Part of him was very hot and burning but inside he seemed to be all chilly and shivery. He rolled off Dead Ernest and stumbled towards the church. He was groaning and holding his head and not looking where he was going.

Round the corner of a high gravestone came Johann Sebastian, the organist's cat. The two animals bumped right into each other. Maximus, being the smallest, fell flat on the ground.

'Sorry, old chap,' mewed Johann, 'but you really should look where you're going. Are you all right? You look very red around the whiskers!'

'I feel dreadful,' moaned Maximus. 'I don't think I can make it back to the vestry.'

'I'll give you a ride,' said the cat. 'Let me hoist you up on my back and I'll soon have you in bed.'

Johann gently lifted Maximus up with one furry paw and put him on his back. 'Grab hold of some fur and then you won't fall off.'

In next to no time Maximus was lying in his bed. The cat had found some cream to put on his sunburn and Maximus was feeling better already. As he lay there he thought to himself, 'I don't deserve this. Johann Sebastian has been so kind to me but I didn't help anyone. Poor Patrick and Paula couldn't go to the gig, Barnabas couldn't go to the hospital and Herbert only wanted me to see his granddaughter. I have not been a very nice mouse today.' He jumped out of bed just in time to let Patrick and Paula go to Willy and the Whisker Bangers.

Heavenly Father,
It is very easy to be selfish — to think always of ourselves before we think of others. Help us to put other people first and ourselves last. Amen.

Road safety last

It was the great day. At last it had come – the day Maximus had been looking forward to for so long. He jumped out of bed and ran to the window. Yes! The sun was shining. Nothing was going to stop it happening. Today would be his day – today he would show them all that he was the best.

It was the day of the Great Skateboard Challenge Race. The animals who lived near the church had entered teams. Maximus was riding a green skateboard in the B.R.M. (British Racing Mice) team. The Shell team had been entered by the snails with Sebastian Slow as rider. No one knew how he would get on as he had no paws to push with. Barnabas was driving the Batmobile and everyone thought he would get off to a flying start. The Fur-aria team skateboard was powered by Robert the operatic rabbit. Finally, Herbert was the rider for the hedgehog team who were known as the Pushing Prickles.

The race was to be twice round the outside of the whole churchyard and was due to start at ten o'clock. By half past nine most of the teams were in the pits – that is

to say, the path between the church and the road. There were baby snails chanting, 'Slow, Slow, quick, quick, Slow', as they crowded round Sebastian. Paula was wiping Maximus' goggles and all her children were shouting, 'Max, Max, we want a Maximum.' Barnabas had yet to arrive. The hedgehogs were all grunting around Herbert who was drinking from a large bottle of milk.

'He thinks it's the Milk Race,' whispered Maximus to Paula.

Just as the clock on the church tower was about to strike ten, Barnabas appeared from round the corner of the church. 'I simply cannot comprehend how anyone with any nocturnal aspirations can possibly be expected to energise themselves at this frightful hour of the day,' said the bat. 'However, I am now prepared for mobilisation and anticipate a totally satisfactory outcome to this little sporting contest.'

'Pardon?' said Robert.

'What?' asked Maximus.

'I think he means he's ready to start,' said Patrick. And he gathered all the competitors round him as he hopped onto a gravestone.

'As the official starter of the Great Skateboard Challenge Race there are a few rules I must bring to your attention. Firstly, I shall disqualify any animal who cheats — either by taking a short cut or by driving dangerously. You must obey the Highway Code when on the roads at all times. You must wear protective clothing. The winner will be the first skateboard to cross the gateway back into the churchyard after going twice round the course. Now get to your positions.'

The animals lined up. The crowd started cheering for their particular favourite. Patrick held up a cap gun and pulled the trigger. The Great Skateboard Challenge Race was on.

The Fur-aria took an early lead with Robert's powerful paws pushing hard on the road surface. The Shell team were shouting at Sebastian who appeared to have gone to sleep inside his shell. Barnabas turned the wrong way out of the gateway and had to do a U-turn to join the race again. Herbert fell off his board and rolled over into the gutter, a great ball of prickles. Maximus kept working very hard and soon was only just behind Robert.

The course led round the churchyard wall towards a road junction. Painted in large letters on the road was the word STOP. Robert, singing at the top of his voice from an opera by Pawccini, stopped at the sign before turning sharply left. Maximus, by this time, was going too fast to stop.

Coming up the road from the right hand side was a pack of cycling frogs out for a ride in the countryside. As Maximus skateboarded over the stop line he ran straight into the leading frog cyclist. Maximus dived off his skateboard and landed on the head of the frog who had toppled from his bike. The frogs who had been pedalling behind the leader rode right into his bike and in turn tumbled on top of Maximus and the front frog. More and more frogs kept landing on the pile until there was a heap of wriggling frogs, and one squashed mouse, all hopping mad at the accident.

Just as the final frog fell from his gleaming mountain bike onto the others so Barnabas and Herbert came straight out of the turning, adding two more skateboards, one hedgehog and one bat, to the heaving pile.

At that moment a loud whistle blew and, gazing up from underneath a wet green frog, Maximus saw Patrick on top of the churchyard wall. He had a piece of grass in his paws and blew through it again to make the piercing whistle sound. Everyone stood, sat or lay still. They all looked at Patrick who, in his loudest and most official voice, shouted, 'Stay still each one of you and pay attention. Maximus, you are disqualified for having failed to obey the Highway Code. You did not stop at the road junction and it was you who caused all this trouble. The race will be rerun later.'

The frogs untangled themselves from each other and from their bikes. Fortunately no one had been badly hurt and they soon set off again. The race was restarted without Maximus and this time there were no accidents. It was very close, but Robert turned out to be the winner and he very kindly shared some of his prize with the others. It had been a great success for everyone but Maximus. But he did learn his lesson about road safety!

Heavenly Father,
So many accidents happen because people are careless. Help all who drive to do so safely. Help us to remember the Highway Code and to behave sensibly on roads. Amen.

Maximus and the robbery

'It's gone!' shouted Maximus. 'It's simply disappeared. It was here only a few minutes ago and now it's gone.'

Maximus and Patrick had just popped out of the church for a few minutes to talk to Herbert the hedgehog in the graveyard. The moment they came back into the building they saw something dreadful had happened. The box near the door, which visitors put money in, had gone. It had been taken off the wall.

'Now what shall I do?' asked Maximus. 'Here am I, the church guard mouse, and almost in front of my whiskers someone has stolen the money box. I shall get the sack — I've failed.'

'No one's going to blame you, Maximus. What matters is that we find out who did it,' said Patrick. 'Let's see if there are any clues?'

'What are clues?' asked his worried friend.

'Clues are what thieves leave when they steal things. It might be a set of paw-prints, or a hanky with their name on, or even a few strands of fur. A detective can work out who the thief was from clues.'

The two mice hunted around for clues. Patrick looked under the pews and Maximus searched among the shelves near the door where the hymnbooks were kept. They found all sorts of odd things like chewing gum stuck under one of the seats, several gloves and a dead umbrella, but there didn't seem to be any clues.

'It's no good,' moaned Maximus. 'There is nothing we can do. We'll never get the money back for the church.'

Just at that moment he saw a few strands of long grey fur caught on the door lock. 'Patrick, look!' he yelled. 'I've found a clue. It's fur — it's grey and it's long and it smells of rabbit. It's got to have been Robert or one of his family. Shall we go and ask him if he did it? Rabbits have bad habits, so my grandma used to say. I always thought he looked slushpickus.'

'The word is suspicious,' laughed Patrick. 'No, we won't go and see Robert. There could be all sorts of reasons for the fur. What we will do is to call Inspector Morse Toad. He's the best detective I know. Let's go and get him now.'

The two mice scampered off to see the police toad. On their way they met Herbert and his family.

'Terrible thing's happened,' said Maximus. 'The money box has been stolen from the church. We've found a clue and I think Robert did it.'

They carried on, leaving the hedgehogs discussing the robbery. A few moments later they met Johann Sebastian, the organist's cat.

'Dreadful news, isn't it, about the money box?' said Maximus to the cat. 'This gang of robbing rabbits has been stealing from churches. Robert's the leader.'

The ground was slippery and quite wet as they got nearer to the small pond where the Inspector and his police force lived. As the mice reached the edge of the water a green, leathery-looking face popped up.

'Evening all,' said Inspector Morse Toad, 'and how can we be of help?'

'Well, Robert the rabbit has stolen the money box from the church, and we thought, that is to say, Patrick thought, that you were the best detective to come and solve the case, even though we've found the clue and we know that Robert done it!' said Maximus, all in one breath.

'Now, slow down, young Maximus,' said the toad as he took out a small notebook from the top pocket of his uniform. 'Tell me again slowly what has happened. I think perhaps, Patrick, you should start.' And between them the two mice told the Inspector all about the robbery.

'I shall need to come and visit the scene of the crime,' said the toad when they had finished.

'But we know Robert did it,' argued Maximus. 'Why don't you go and a vest him?'

'Arrest him, you mean. I shan't do that until I am quite sure that he was the thief. In the meantime I suggest you do not go around telling everyone that a certain rabbit did it. That has not been proved. I shall take a police tracker frog with me.'

The toad, the tracker frog, and the two mice went to the church. The Inspector was carrying a small case with him. He took out some white powder and sprinkled it on the wall where the box had been. Maximus could see that it helped the paw prints to show up clearly. Morse Toad then searched the back of the church. He looked at the fur caught in the door lock and then he spoke to the mice.

'I think I've seen all I need to here. I shall continue my enquiries elsewhere and will let you know what happens.' The toad and frog hopped off leaving the two mice chatting about the robbery.

The next day Inspector Morse Toad returned to the church with Robert the rabbit.

'So it was him,' said Maximus. 'I knew I was right. I could be a really great detective.'

'Just watch what you're saying,' said the police toad sternly. 'I have come to speak to a thief. That thief is you, Maximus.'

'But, but, but . . . I never stole anything,' said the very worried mouse.

'Oh yes, you did. You stole something very precious. You stole Robert's good name. You went round telling everyone that he was a thief. Well, Robert is not a thief. He did not take the money box. It was the vicar of the church who came in to take it away to empty it — something you might have thought of if you hadn't been so keen to blame poor Robert.'

'Oh dear,' cried Maximus. 'What have I done now? I didn't mean to steal your good name, Robert. I'm very sorry because I know you're a very good rabbit. Please forgive me. What can I do?'

'I suggest you go and tell everyone you saw yesterday that you were wrong and that Robert did not steal the money. In future be careful how you talk about other animals. Now it's up to Robert.'

'Maximus, I forgive you, but never do it again,' said the rabbit kindly. 'You can hurt animals very badly by what you say. Promise me you will think before you squeak!'

Heavenly Father,
It is so easy to say wrong things about people. Help us to know what the truth is and to be ready to speak it at all times. Amen.